The Mountain's Blood

by

Lari Don

Illustrated by Paul Duffield

700037789426

D1148542

To my own kickass heroine,
Trina Miller PhD, who introduced me to
Inanna, then stood well back!

First published in 2011 in Great Britain by
Barrington Stoke Ltd
18 Walker St, Edinburgh, EH3 7LP

www.barringtonstoke.co.uk

ISBN: 978-1-84299-400-9

Printed in Great Britain by Bell & Bain Ltd

Contents

Chapter 1
The Axe In My Wardrobe

I opened my wardrobe and an axe fell out, just missing my toes.

"Goddess of *Love*! Yuck! Why do I have to be Goddess of *Love*? I'll never get to use my axe when I'm just Goddess of *Love*."

I chucked the axe back into the wardrobe, and dragged out the nearest dress. Then I slammed the wardrobe door shut, so I could get dressed without seeing the dusty pile of weapons at the back.

I still had a scowl on my face when I left my room, so when my brother Utu the Sun God saw me, he smiled his big shiny grin. "Cheer up, little sister Inanna. Isn't *love* meant to make you happy?"

I ran off towards the court-yard of the House of the Gods. I had to squeeze past a crowd of cousins watching a wrestling match between my uncles Enki, God of Wisdom and Water, and Enlil, God of Storms.

Everyone else in the family had a much cooler god-job. It must be a lot more fun to control the sea or the storms than be in charge of *love* ...

As I passed the great hall, I heard a loud voice shaking the walls. It was Anu, the boss God of Heaven and Sky himself, yelling orders at the rest of the family from behind his big beard. I bowed to him as I walked past, but he didn't notice me.

It was calm in the stables. There were no other gods there. Just me and my seven blue bulls. I dragged them out of their stalls, keeping away from their horns and hooves. I tied them to my chariot, leapt in, and ordered them to gallop out of the stables.

And I rode across the sky, like I did every day.

I could see all the world below me. The long rivers flowing, the bright sands blowing, the wet marshes glinting. The flowers and reeds, trees and grain growing. The lions and eagles hunting. The farmers and shepherds working.

My fingers loosened their grip on the reins and I smiled. The world was beautiful under my bulls' hooves and my chariot's wheels.

I do love the world, and everything that grows there.

We flew over my very own city, Uruk. I watched my people bowing down to me and bringing gifts to my temples.

I do love being worshipped.

Oh, alright. I'm an old softie really. I admit I do love the world I see every day. Love can be fine. In its place.

I smiled, I watched the world, and I loved it.

But then I saw in front of me, between the biggest bull's curved blue horns, a dark stain where the land met the sky. A filthy mark on my world.

"I must see what that is." I flicked the reins and the bulls galloped faster.

As we got nearer, I saw it was a pile of rocks. No, just one rock. One massive rock. One high rocky mountain.

But it couldn't be. There have never been any mountains this far south. It couldn't be a mountain.

Chapter 2
The Shadow of the Mountain

We flew closer.

It *was* a mountain! Huge and high and grey.

But there wasn't a mountain here the last time I flew this way. Surely I'd have noticed something this *huge*?

The mountain's vast shadow darkened miles of land. The ground around was

covered with grit and ash. Swirls of smoke blocked the sun from fields and flowers.

We flew slowly round the mountain, looking at the damage caused by its shadow and its ash.

The green grass, the singing birds, the whistling reeds and the rich flocks were all choked and dying.

There were many paths cutting through the land, away from the mountain. Paths cut by escaping deer, goats, and sheep. Paths cut by the farmers and shepherds who love me, taking their families and running away.

Away from my land. Away from *me*.

I couldn't let this mountain empty my land.

I steered the bulls even closer, until the soot burnt my nostrils, and I called out –

"Mountain!"

There was no answer.

I shouted though the smoky air –

"*Mountain!*"

There was no answer at all.

"My name is Inanna, Goddess of ..."

I stopped. Was 'Goddess of Love' going to impress a mountain this big and solid?

Possibly not.

I tried again.

"Mountain, I am the Goddess Inanna!"

The mountain said nothing.

"Mountain, you are growing too tall, you are destroying this good green land with your shadow and your smoke. You must stop."

The mountain shrugged its stony shoulders. Rocks rolled down its bumpy back to the ground.

The mountain *shrugged*! At *me*!

"I am the Goddess Inanna. Bow down to me!"

The mountain did not listen to me.

"You will bow down to me now!" I spoke slowly, clearly. So there could be no mistake. "Bow down flat so you wipe your nose on the ground and press your lips to the earth! Bow down NOW!"

I waited. The mountain did not move.

I waited. The mountain stayed still as stone.

I waited. The mountain did not bow. It did not wipe its nose on the ground. It did not press its lips to the earth.

Shivering with anger, I turned my back on the mountain, and ordered my bulls home. But I would not forget this mountain. I could not forget that it had shrugged at me. That it would not bow down to me. I would come back, and this mountain *would* bow to me.

Chapter 3
Stars On My Fore-head

By the time I got home, I knew what to do.

Maybe the mountain didn't know who I was. Maybe it didn't understand about gods. Perhaps it was hard to hear through all that stone. Perhaps it was hard to think with all that rock inside its head.

So the next time the mountain saw me, it would see a goddess in all her glory.

I opened my wardrobe again. I took out a longer dress, with even more layers, in thinner, lighter fabric.

I brushed my hair until it gleamed, long and wavy like Anu's beard.

I opened my wooden box of paints and pastes.

I smoothed shine of amber on my lips.

I drew black of night around my eyes.

I rubbed perfumed oil on my wrists.

I opened my silver chest of jewels.

I pushed rings of gold on each finger.

I hung beads of blood around my neck.

And last, I put stars on my fore-head.

Bright with jewels and smelling of riches. I walked down the cloudy steps of our high house to the world below.

I said to myself, *I am the Goddess of Love. Someone must love me enough to follow me all the way to the mountain.*

I walked in long earth-swallowing strides to my own city, Uruk.

I stood tall, spread my arms and summoned those who love me. And they all came! The men, the women, the children, calling out their love for me.

I led my followers, dancing and singing, towards the mountain. I led them through the smoke, the ash and the heat. I led them past the twisted burnt bodies of animals and people who hadn't run from the mountain fast enough.

A lion walked beside me.

A scorpion clung to my sandal.

An eagle flew above me.

A line of people snaked after me.

I arrived at the mountain. My beauty glittered even in its dull shadow.

I called on my people to bow to me. They cheered and they bowed. They pressed their faces in the hot ash for me.

I shouted up to the mountain, "See how easy it is! See how happy they are to bow to me, to the Goddess of Love! Now you bow to me and give me your love."

There was a pause.

We all watched the mountain.

The lion. The scorpion. The eagle. We watched the mountain.

The people lifted their burnt, sore faces, and watched the mountain.

I called again, "Bow down to me!"

The mountain shifted and creaked.

Yes! It was going to bow down to me. It had seen my glory, my power.

Then the mountain ...

Burped!

It burped a cloud of rude greasy smoke right at me and my followers.

Then its belly rumbled. Was it going to burp again? My followers leapt up in fear and fled, coughing and spitting.

Leaving me alone. My dress burnt. My hair stinking of smoke. My jewels and stars covered in ash.

I walked away. Glad the mountain's shadow hid me from the gaze of heaven, and from the House of the Gods.

Chapter 4
Asking Nicely

I ran through the corridors of the House of the Gods, hoping no one would see me trailing ash and blowing my nose. But I heard someone snigger. Maybe my brother, who sees everything from his place in the sky.

I fell onto my bed, hiding my face in the blankets.

It had burped at me. That mountain had actually burped at me!

Ignoring a goddess is bad enough. But burping at a goddess is a big mistake.

I would go back to the mountain, but this time I would take an army with me. That big bully of a mountain could turn its back on me, but it could not ignore my whole family.

So I got up, I found a clean dress, I polished my jewels, I shined my stars, I smoothed my hair, I washed and painted my face, and I picked the scorpion off my sandal.

Now I looked splendid enough for a feast of the gods. But perhaps I should take a gift as well. Something sweet and warm and tasty. I should take the god Anu's favourite pudding!

I went to the kitchens. I baked a cake with butter and barley. I sliced honey cheese. I mixed date syrup.

Then, with a heavy plate in my hands, I walked to the great hall of the gods. To ask the men with the cool god-jobs for their help with this insulting mountain.

My seat in the great hall was near the door, at the bottom of the table.

I am, after all, only the Goddess of Love.

I walked past my chair, and kept going to the top of the table.

I twirled and swirled round the thrones of my uncles and cousins, fluttering my eyelashes, smiling sweetly until I stood beside the high throne of Anu, the head god.

I spoke over the noise of the feast. "Anu, my lord."

I bowed as far down as I could without the stars slipping over my eye-brows, and I offered the cake to Anu.

Anu turned slowly to look at me. "Yes?" He'd never seen me at this end of the table before.

"Anu, highest of all the gods, I've come to ask for your help.

"There's a mountain below, destroying the land. It blocks out the sun, so the grass will not grow, so the sheep die, so the people who worship us leave our land. But the mountain will not stop getting taller."

Anu shrugged at me, his great black curly beard rippling on his chest.

Maybe he didn't understand how important this was.

I bowed again. Down. Further. As far as I had ever bowed. A star slipped off my forehead and shattered on the floor.

I stood up straight. "Anu. This mountain refused to bow. It refused to bow to *me*!"

I stamped my foot. I heard my brother laugh, so I took a deep breath and tried to smile. "It refused to bow to me, but it would not dare refuse you, Anu. It would bow right to the ground if *you* told it to."

I turned to face them all, and shouted down the table. "Come with me, my family, and teach this mountain how to respect the gods. Teach it to wipe its nose on the ground and press its lips to the earth."

I hoped they would leap up, whooping and hot-blooded, keen to teach the mountain a lesson. But they didn't move. Some of my cousins looked down at the table. Others looked up at Anu. Not one of them met my eyes.

The hall was silent.

"Please?" I smiled. "Pretty please?"

Still no one looked at me. All my make-up and jewellery and clean clothes were wasted if no one would even look at me.

I turned back to Anu. "Please, king of all the gods, come with me and teach this mountain how to respect us."

Anu frowned. "We have seen that mountain. It is a long way below us. It cannot hurt us."

"It hurts the land," I said loudly. "And it does not recognise my power, our power."

He looked away. "That mountain has its own power."

I was shocked. Anu never admitted anything or anyone else was as powerful as him. Perhaps I hadn't heard him right.

"But, Anu, you aren't afraid of the mountain's power?"

Anu didn't answer. For a moment I was afraid too.

But I raised my voice to the roof. "Are you *all* afraid of its power?"

Anu said firmly, "We are safe from the mountain up here. We do not choose to challenge the mountain. We prefer not to anger it. Leave the mountain alone."

I shook my head. I couldn't believe what I was hearing.

This mountain wasn't showing us respect, and gods must have respect, or we have no power.

This mountain was damaging our world, killing our plants, our animals and our people.

And this mountain was a danger to our home, our safety, our future. Couldn't Anu see that?

So I said, clear and slow as if I were speaking to the mountain:

"If we do not make it bow down now, how long before its greasy smoke and rocky shoulders reach as high as your sky, Anu? How long will it leave us alone if it thinks we're afraid of it?"

Anu slammed his fist on the table. "We are safe here. The mountain does not bother us."

"It bothers me!" I yelled back. "I will not hide up here and be insulted by a lump of rock. If you won't fight it, then I will. That mountain will bow down to me, and me alone!"

Then I ran from the hall, stepping on the fallen cake, and ripping the hem of my dress.

Chapter 5

What Else Do I Keep In My Wardrobe?

I pulled so hard on the handle of my wardrobe that the door fell off.

I threw the door into a corner, and reached into the wardrobe.

This time I didn't take out a dress. This time I pulled out:

My armour. As light on my strong shoulders as fifty feathers, but hard enough to stop the horns of a charging bull.

My arrows and my long, curved bow.

My javelin. Weighted for throwing, sharpened to kill.

My spear. Heavier than the javelin, but solid and steady in my fist.

My lance. Longer than the spear and the javelin joined, for driving through an enemy's chest.

My mace. A jagged hammer to crush bones.

My sword. Cold and smooth, for hacking and slicing.

And last of all, my sharp axe. To whirl and whistle above my head, then cut down anyone who stands against me.

It was too long since I'd used my weapons, so I ripped the hem right off my dress and used it to give them a quick polish.

I looked at the gleaming line of metal blades, edges and points, and smiled. Not a polite great hall smile, but the smile of a lion looking forward to the hunt.

I pulled off my jewels, and dropped my stars into a black box. I didn't need to shine, because I wasn't trying to impress the mountain any more.

I changed out of my torn, dirty robes into the bright beautiful dress of battle.

I put the sword in my belt, the bow and arrows on my back, and gathered the handles of the other weapons into my arms like a woman gathering a harvest of reeds.

Chapter 6

Thanks for Nothing, Big Brother

I struggled into the corridor with my armful of weapons. I felt warm air at my back and my brother Utu said, "Can I help you with those, sister?"

I turned round, dropped the weapons on his toes, and yelled at him, "Fat lot of help you were, laughing at me in there!"

"Sorry, but you weren't going to win against Anu. I wasn't going to join you when you were losing."

I scowled at him. "And why didn't you tell us about that mountain? You shine on everything in the world, you must have seen it grow. Why didn't you tell anyone?"

"I did tell the family, one night when you were at a temple in Uruk being worshipped. But by the time we realised it was still growing, it was too big to fight. So they found excuses. *It's not our problem. We don't want to annoy it.*"

"But you agree it must bow to us?"

He shrugged. "I agree it's damaging the land. There are farms and gardens I haven't reached with my sun rays for weeks. And I agree it's proud and dangerous, so if everyone were ordered to fight it I would add my fire to the battle."

"But will you help *me* fight it?" I asked.

"Sister, I am the sun. That mountain will never reach high enough to hurt me. But Anu is the Sky God. My path runs through his sky every day. He can make life very difficult for me. It's dangerous for me to go against him."

I spoke softly. "Do you remember when we were children, when we learnt to use these weapons together? Will you fight with me one more time?"

He looked at the floor. "Do you think you can win?"

"I'm going to try. And if I don't win, will anyone care? Will anyone notice that the chair at the very end of the table is empty? That no one in the world loves any more? But I will try to win. And I'd have more chance with another warrior by my side. Brother, will you help me?"

"No." He sighed. "I will not stand against Anu. But I will watch over you, and I will tell the tale of your battle to our family, so they do notice you and what you have done. I promise you that."

That was the most I would get from the golden boy of the family. A witness and a story. A story of victory or defeat.

My brother helped carry my weapons to the gate of heaven. He waved his hands over them, and the edges, points and blades shone even sharper.

Then he turned his back on me. I felt a cold shadow touch my skin.

Chapter 7
Blades at the Door of Heaven

I stood at the wide door of heaven, my weapons at my feet, and I kicked the door open. I yelled, "Mountain, bow down to me!"

The mountain shrugged. Rocks rolled and rumbled down its sides.

I wasn't really surprised.

"Bow down to me, wipe your nose on the ground, press your lips to the Earth."

It shrugged again.

This mountain had ignored me in my bull chariot. It had ignored me with my followers. Now it ignored me and my line of weapons.

I would *force* this mountain to obey me.

I lifted my bow and took careful aim at the very top of the mountain. I sent a swarm of arrows speeding to the summit of my enemy.

I stood on the edge of heaven and saw every single arrow burn in the wet red heat at the heart of the mountain.

I roared in shock and anger.

I lifted my javelin, held it balanced in my hand, and threw it at the neck of the mountain.

My throw was perfect, rising and falling like the curve of a rainbow. But the point of the javelin shattered as it hit the mountain.

I took the thicker, heavier spear. I threw it with all my strength at the back-bone of the mountain, my feet lifting off the ground after it. The spear's blade hit the spine of the mountain, but the spine held and the blade cracked.

I picked up my mace, the head carved to cause fear, the handle carved to give grip, and I threw it end over end at the ribs of the mountain.

I heard a wonderful crunch as the mace hit its broad target. But the crunch was the mace head being crushed by the impact.

I was running out of weapons. But I still had my axe. Nothing could stand against my axe. I stroked the moon-curved blade, curled

my fingers round the handle, and whirled the axe above my head.

I heard it whistle and I let it go, hoping it would cut deep into the mountain's skull. But my axe bounced off the cliff face, and tumbled and clattered all the way down to the feet of the mountain. It lay on the ground, scraped, scratched and blunted.

I screamed with fury, and I grabbed my lance.

With the wooden length of the lance held firmly under my arm, my steady hand aimed the metal point at my enemy's belly.

And I leapt from the door of heaven.

I followed the pure line of the lance, slicing apart the blue of Anu's sky.

The lance struck the mountain straight and true, but it shivered and split along its length. As it fell into splinters in my fist, I slammed into the side of the mountain.

Chapter 8
The Last Chance

I rolled and leapt to my feet. I ran to the top of the mountain, my legs strong and my head high. I stood at the summit, and reached towards the sky.

"Now I stand higher than you, mountain. So bow down to me!"

But the mountain ignored me. It had broken all of my weapons, and still it ignored me.

I looked down at the grey shadow on the ground below. The crust of dust and ash over the green fields. The empty farms and twisted bodies.

I drew my sun-sharp sword from my waist. I raised the blade and I stabbed it deep into the heart of the mountain. I roared in triumph.

Then I felt my sword get lighter and lighter, as the blade melted and dripped from the hilt. My sword was swallowed by the mountain.

I stood there on the very top of the mountain. With no weapons. Empty handed. Totally defeated.

But I am a goddess. So I said in a slow, calm voice, "Mountain, this is your last chance. Bow down to me. Wipe your nose on the ground, press your lips to the earth."

The mountain spat hot metal bubbles of my melted sword back at me. I ducked as the boiling drops struck my armour. The heat burnt through to my skin. I hissed in pain and I ran. I turned away and I ran down the mountain.

Chapter 9
The Last Laugh

As it felt my feet running down its sides, the mountain laughed.

It laughed! At *me*!

I felt giggles and chuckles rippling across its rocky sides. It laughed and laughed, and its rocks rolled merrily down to the dead grey ground.

The boulders bounced joyfully past me. So I held out my arms, caught a boulder in each hand, and I laughed too.

I lifted the two rocks high above my head, and I crashed them down. Crashed them hard into the stony skin of the mountain.

I bashed and battered and bruised the mountain with its own rocks and stones.

I forced the mountain's solid power to fight against itself.

I hit hard and heavy and again and again.

My nails broke, my fingers bled, my arms grew tired, but I did not stop.

I did not stop even when my rocky weapons fell apart.

Because when the mountain had shrugged at me and laughed at me, it had shaken loose hundreds of rocks and stones. I could run to the feet of the mountain and find as many weapons as I wanted. Perfect weapons left there by the mountain itself.

When the boulder in my left hand broke into small pebbles, I ran to the feet of the mountain to grab another boulder, and used it to smash and shatter more ridges and ribs.

When the rock in my right hand crumbled into sand, I ran down to choose another rock, which I thumped and thudded against the mountain's slopes and sides.

I battered and I bashed until the mountain began to bleed.

Until dribbles of red hot rock squeezed from narrow cracks.

Until streams of the mountain's blood flowed from deep gullies and ravines.

Until rivers of the mountain's life poured from long valleys.

I did not stop even when I had to jump high in the air to prevent my legs being cooked by the mountain's blood.

I did not stop even when my sandals burnt under my feet.

I bashed with boulders and struck with rocks until the mountain shook and shivered under me.

When I felt its weakness at last, I dropped my weapons. I laid my hands on its warm grey skin, I gripped its stony bones and I wrestled that mountain to the ground.

Chapter 10
The Shadow Shrinks

I felt my enemy fall away beneath my feet, then I danced along the mountain's long spine as it lay flat on the ground.

I bellowed, "Now you bow down to me, now you wipe your nose on the ground, now you press your lips to the earth! Now your shadow is small and your smoke is cooling."

I licked the ash off my lips, and wiped the blood from my finger-tips.

I watched from the low spine of the mountain as its smoke blew away and the sun, my brother, shone again on the land.

I took deep breaths of fresh air. The grass grew, and the lambs leapt, a lion stretched and yawned, and a crow flapped to a tree.

I smiled as the farmers and shepherds walked home through wisps of smoke. They bowed their heads to me, and gave me gifts.

They gave me gifts of fresh food and new shining weapons.

When night fell on the clean land, my bulls came to fetch me in my chariot.

And I went to a feast.

Chapter 11

Dressed in Blood and Ashes

I went to the great hall of the gods. But I didn't bother washing my face or putting pretty clothes on. I didn't fix stars to my fore-head or bake cakes for anyone.

I marched into the great hall stinking of smoke and sweat, with burnt eye-brows and battered armour. I swung my new axe in my bloody hands.

Now, my family all looked at me. There was silence, until I kicked over the low chair of the Goddess of Love.

When the sounds of that crash died away, there was deeper silence. I pushed past my brother and my uncles with their cool god-jobs. I walked to the top of the table, and I sat down beside the god Anu.

I sat in the high throne of the Goddess of War. I listened as my brother told my family what the sun had seen, how the Goddess had brought down the mountain.

And I have sat in the high throne of the Goddess of War at every feast and council since. With my axe, sharp in the sunlight, by my hand.

I kept the Goddess of Love job as well, because no one else wanted it, but I don't mind so much, now I can use my axe sometimes too.

The First Words and the Last Word

From the hand of Inanna, Goddess of War and of Love, to my new followers

The northern story-teller Lari Don has woven her own tale about the day I wrestled a mountain and won. But the first time I heard this story told was at least 5,000 years ago.

Thousands of years ago I was worshipped in the land of Sumeria, which is now southern Iraq. The people of Sumeria told tales of my battle with a mountain, tales of how I won (or stole) even more cool god-jobs, and tales of how I went down to the underworld and lived. They told the stories, they sang them, they made them into poems, they even wrote them down.

In fact, the people of Sumeria may have been the first people to write anything down, because they invented the earliest writing ever found.

They wrote my family's stories (as well as letters, laws, library lists, and school lessons) on clay tablets. The earliest known poet, a woman called Enheduanna, wrote poems in honour of me.

I was their Goddess of Love but I also won many other powers. By the end of my rule, the armies of Sumeria were carrying my flag into battle. They worshipped me, loved me and feared me as the Goddess of War.

But then my family and our stories vanished. The clay tablets of our tales were buried under the sand for thousands of years.

I am one of the oldest known goddesses – older than the Greek goddesses or the Viking goddesses. It wouldn't be wise to call me 'ancient' though, because I still look pretty good and I still swing a mean axe. But no one read my stories again until those lost clay tablets were found in Iraq just over 100 years ago.

However, I was never completely forgotten. You may not have heard of me until you read this book, and there may be no temples to me now, but I am not powerless. For there are still no high mountains in my homeland.

The mountains are still afraid of me. Are you?

BATTLE CARDS

Lari Don

Author

Favourite heroine:
Ninshubur, Inanna's servant, who defeats even more Sumerian monsters than the goddess does!

Favourite monster:
Fenrir, a world-destroying Viking wolf.

Your weapon of choice:
A round shield with a sharpened rim — attack and defence in one!

Favourite fight scene:
The second duel between Jen and Shu Lien in *Crouching Tiger, Hidden Dragon*.

Goodie or Baddie:
My characters think I'm a baddie, because I'm always putting them in danger!

RELOADED

Paul Duffield

Illustrator

Favourite heroine:
Achilles.
Favourite monster:
The Balrog.
Your weapon of choice:
Katana.
Favourite fight scene:
Ziyi Zhang vs. Michelle Yeoh in
Crouching Tiger, Hidden Dragon
Special secret power:
Hiten Mitsurugi Ryu!
Goodie or Baddie:
Chaotic Neutral!

RELOADED

Barrington Stoke would like to thank all its readers for commenting on the manuscript before publication and in particular:

Usmann Ahmed
Charley Barnes
Ryan Brooks
Oliver Carter
Dominique
Latham Eggleston
Lucas Farrimond
Linda Flynn
Michael Forsyth
Maisy Gibbs
Crystal Hannam
Ziaul Hoque
Charlie Henson
Leonora Hussey
Anika Hussain
Thomas Irish
Sara Kelly
Kamran Khalid
Ramith Kumaradas

Shauna Ledger
Rachal Mallard
Travis McLuckie
Sophie-Marie Page-Newman
Toby North
Ben Pearce
Rushil Pithia
Jacob Reardon
Harrison Reeves
David Savoury
Stewart Scott
Bethany Searles
Jarvis Silvester
Mrs Short
Hemal Soni
Chris Stecko
Meggie Voce
Leah Woods

Become a Consultant!

Would you like to be a consultant? Ask your parent, carer or teacher to contact us at the email address below – we'd love to hear from them! They can also find out more by visiting our website.

schools@barringtonstoke.co.uk
www.barringtonstoke.co.uk

TAM O SHANTER

BY
LARI DON

A scream shatters the moonlit night.

Tam has seen what no one should see.

And they know it.

Hell has broken loose.

Fears you can't name. Nightmares come real.

And they are out to get him.

Cam Tam outrun death?

THE JAWS OF DEATH
BY
MALACHY DOYLE

Kwang-Su is brave and strong. He will have to be.

He has a long way to go.

Across rivers full of man-eating fish.

Past swamps filled with angry alligators.

At least there aren't any dragons.

Or are there?

You can order *The Jaws of Death* directly from
www.barringtonstoke.co.uk